Fun with Mom

by Ruth Mattison

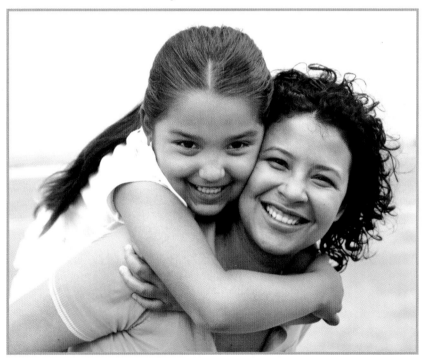

PIONEER VALLEY EDUCATIONAL PRESS, INC.

My mom is cooking.

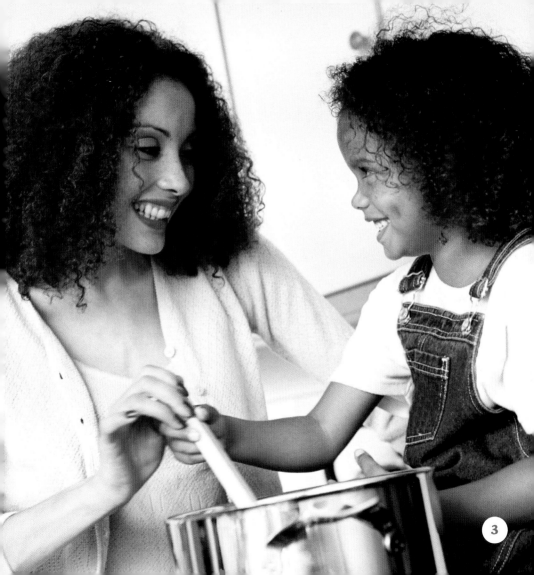

My mom is running.

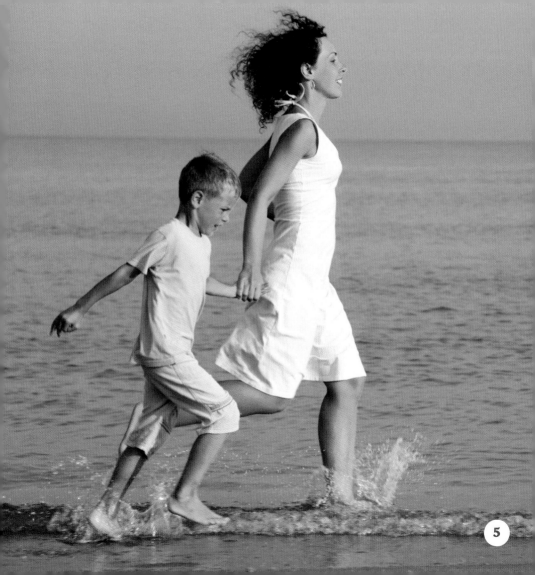

My mom is working.

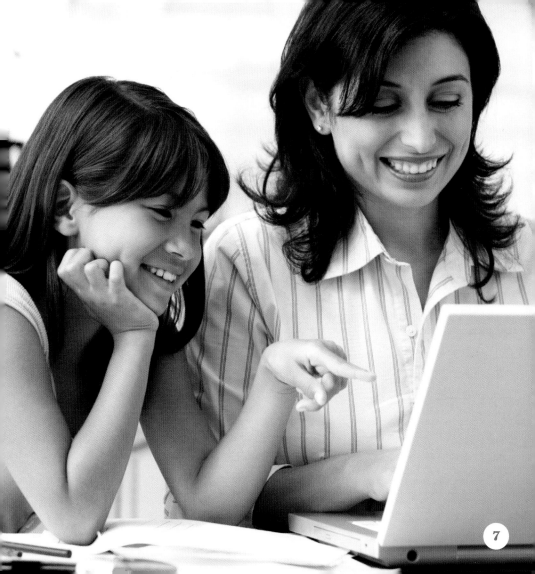

My mom is jumping.

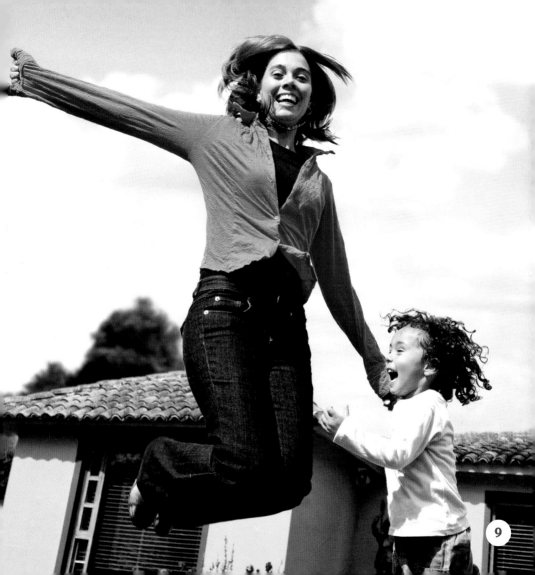

My mom is singing.

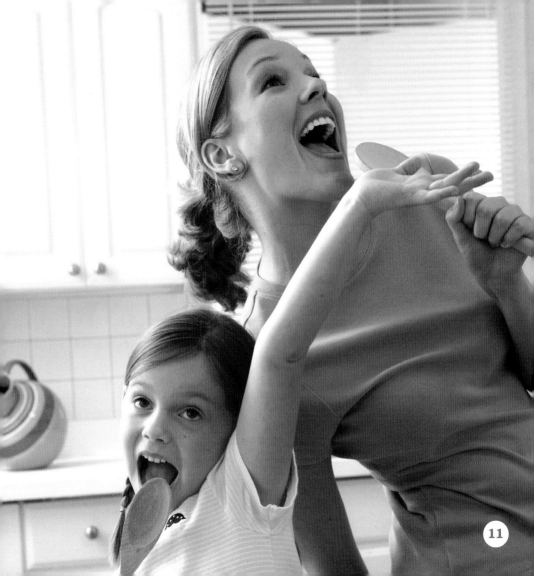

My mom is dancing.

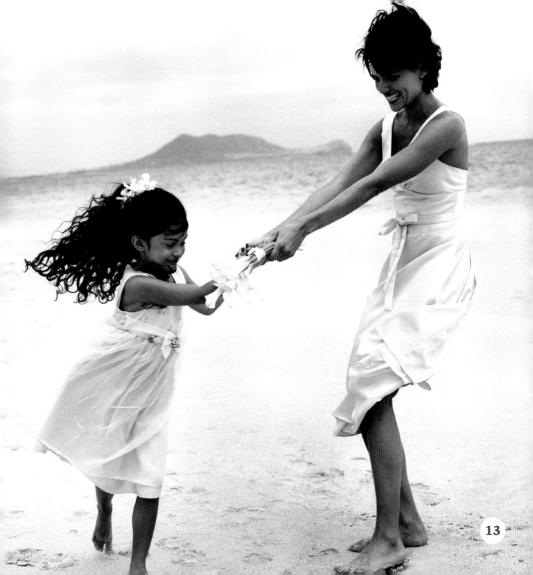

My mom is raking.

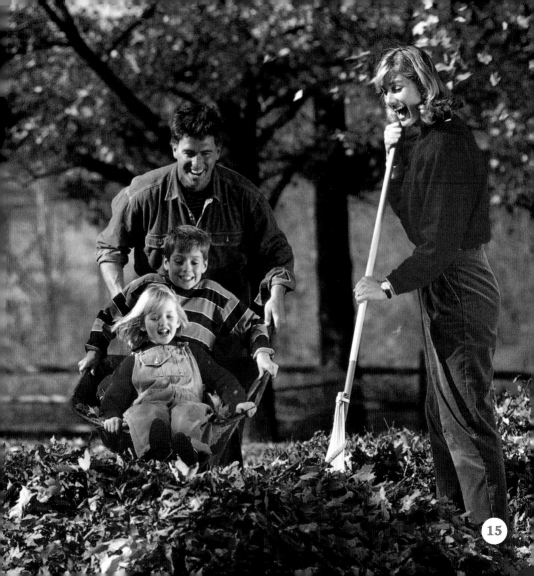

My mom is reading to me.